Chilling
with the
Great Ones

For Judith and Zack. The truth is out there.
—*D.G.*

weirdplanet 3

Chilling with the Great Ones

by Dan Greenburg
illustrated by Macky Pamintuan

A STEPPING STONE BOOK™

Random House   New York

Published in the United States by Random House Children's Books,
a division of Random House, Inc., New York.

RANDOM HOUSE and colophon are registered trademarks and
A STEPPING STONE BOOK and colophon are trademarks of
Random House, Inc.

www.steppingstonesbooks.com
www.randomhouse.com/kids

Educators and librarians, for a variety of teaching tools, visit us at
www.randomhouse.com/teachers

Library of Congress Cataloging-in-Publication Data
Greenburg, Dan.
Chilling with the Great Ones / by Dan Greenburg ;
illustrated by Macky Pamintuan. — 1st ed.
p.   cm. — (Weird planet ; 3)
"A Stepping Stone Book."
SUMMARY: When siblings Klatu, Lek, and Ploo from the planet Loogl return to
the mysterious Area 51 to recover their wrecked spaceship, they meet the Great
Ones—four legendary Looglings who crashed in Roswell sixty years earlier.
ISBN-13: 978-0-375-83346-5 (pbk.) — ISBN-13: 978-0-375-93346-2 (lib. bdg.)
ISBN-10: 0-375-83346-3 (pbk.) — ISBN-10: 0-375-93346-8 (lib. bdg.)
[1. Extraterrestrial beings—Fiction. 2. Brothers and sisters—Fiction. 3. Area 51
(Nev.)—Fiction. 4. Science fiction. 5. Humorous stories.] I. Pamintuan, Macky, ill.
II. Title. III. Series: Greenburg, Dan. Weird planet ; 3.
PZ7.G8278Chi 2006
[E]—dc22   2006001556

Printed in the United States of America
10 9 8 7 6 5 4 3 2 1
First Edition

Contents

Between a Rock and a Sandy Place

VRRRRRRRROOOOOOOOOOOOOMMMM!

The long pink Cadillac with the sharky fins sped through the Nevada desert, kicking up clouds of dust. The sound of its engine shattered the night. The noise sent small creatures skittering across the sand.

"Ooooh, did you see that gizzard run away from us?" shouted Klatu.

"A *gizzard* is part of a bird's stomach," said Lek. "You meant *lizard*."

"I *said lizard*," snapped Klatu.

"You said *gizzard*," said Lek.

"*Lizard*," said Klatu.

Up ahead, beside a gigantic rock formation, was a cluster of bright lights. They came from several army trucks, a crane, and a flatbed truck. Their headlights were trained on something round, metallic, and saucer-shaped.

"Oh no!" said Ploo from the backseat of the pink Cadillac. "What are they doing with our spaceship?"

Ploo had lovely gray skin, huge black eyes, and a large head with a single antenna curling out of it. Her older brother Lek and their even older brother, Klatu, were next to her.

They had sneaked away to Earth from planet Loogl to do extra-credit science projects for school, but Klatu had messed up and crash-landed their spaceship in the desert. Guards from Area 51 had captured Ploo and taken her to the army base. Luckily a little human girl named Lily helped her escape.

"Didn't y'all tell me you made your spacecraft invisible?" asked Jo-Jo. She was their new human friend, and she was driving them in her big pink Cadillac.

"Yes," said Ploo. "With something we call a hide-a-craft. But the humans must have found it." She glared at Klatu and Lek. They had left the hide-a-craft behind in the desert.

"We have to get out of here before they see us!" said Lek. "They will take us prisoner like they did Ploo. Maybe do horrible medical tests on us. Pull off our fingers. Stick things up our *crozzfozzn*."

"You kids better hide," said Jo-Jo. "Can y'all fit under the seats?"

"I have a better idea," said Klatu. "We can morph into human shape. We are experts now at looking like humans. Ready, Lek? Ready, Ploo?"

The three alien kids grew outward and upward. Their heads got smaller. Their arms and legs got thicker. Their eyes shrank down to the beady little things that humans have.

For their human forms, they had chosen haircuts and clothes they'd seen in their

Earthling Studies textbooks. But their text-books were old. Very old. They'd picked old-fashioned sailor suits. Button-up shoes. Straw hats with ribbons.

Jo-Jo looked at their outfits and shook her head. "Some experts," she said.

Their human forms wouldn't last more than an *arp*. They set the *arp*-timers on their wrists. One *arp* of Loogl time was about the same as one hour of Earth time. There were fifty *mynts* to an *arp*. Fifty *mynts* till they began looking like aliens again.

"The flavor of my English gum is fad-ing," said Lek. "Give me another quickly or I am doomed."

Klatu gave each of them another green gum ball. The flavor of English gum only lasted an *arp*. When the flavor faded, they'd hardly be able to speak English at all.

As the kids chewed, Jo-Jo whipped the steering wheel hard to the left. The big pink car swerved into a sharp turn on the highway. Lek, Ploo, and Klatu were thrown against the opposite door.

"What was that?" said Klatu.

"U-turn," said Jo-Jo.

"You want *me* to turn?" said Klatu. He moved so he was facing backward, looking out the rear window. "How is this?"

No sooner had the car turned around than they got an unpleasant surprise. A huge black SUV had pulled up behind them and was blocking the road.

"Where did *that* come from?" said Ploo.

The driver got out of the giant car. He wore a dark trench coat, and above his mouth was a mustache that looked like a caterpillar.

"It is Marcel!" said Klatu.

"We are doomed!" cried Lek.

Marcel had been stalking them since they'd won bags of money in Las Vegas. The casino boss was sure the kids had been cheating. He had sent Marcel after them to prove it.

Jo-Jo made another U-turn, but it was too late. The soldiers had spotted the pink Cadillac. They surrounded both the Caddy and Marcel's car. A soldier came over to Jo-Jo's side of the car. He was wearing a helmet and mirrored sunglasses, even though it was night.

"This is a secured area, ma'am," said the soldier. "You people are trespassing."

"Secured area, my *foot*," said Jo-Jo. "It's just a stretch of empty desert, hon."

"It's a secured area *now*," said the soldier.

"Why?" said Jo-Jo. "Because of that spacecraft?"

"What spacecraft?" said the soldier. "I don't see any spacecraft. But I *would* like to see your driver's license."

Jo-Jo laughed in his face.

"What for?" she asked. "Are you gonna give me a traffic ticket?"

"No, ma'am," said the soldier. "I'm going to take you all back to my commander at the base for questioning."

"And when you do," said Marcel, walking up to the Cadillac, "ask them how they cheated at the roulette wheel at the Titanic Hotel."

"Who the heck are *you*?" asked the soldier.

"My name is Marcel Duchamp and I work for the Titanic Hotel," said Marcel.

"Well, Marcel, I'm taking you back for questioning, too," said the soldier. "As far as I can tell, you're *all* trespassing."

"This is the end of us," whispered Lek. "We shall never see Loogl again!"

A Familiar Paine

Major Paine looked up from the papers on his desk as the soldiers brought Jo-Jo, Klatu, Lek, Ploo, and Marcel into his office.

"Major Paine, sir," said one of the soldiers, "we arrested these people in a secured area out in the desert tonight."

"You rest us," said Klatu, "and yet we are not tired. Why is that?"

"We're not *resting* you," said the soldier, "we're *ar*-resting you. It means we're taking you into *custody*. Do you know what *custody* is?"

"Of course I know what *custardy* is," said Klatu. "*Custardy* is a kind of dessert."

The soldier looked like he was getting a bad headache.

Then Major Paine noticed Jo-Jo. "Well, well," he said. "Welcome back, Jo-Jo."

"Howdy, Major," said Jo-Jo.

"Sir, you *know* this woman?" asked the soldier.

"Heck, yes," said the major. "Jo-Jo was one of our finest aircraft mechanics. She just found it hard to follow orders."

"Major," said Jo-Jo, "these kids are my niece and nephews from back east. I've been showin' 'em the sights around Vegas. Tonight we were drivin' in the desert and we stopped when we saw the spacecraft."

"What spacecraft?" said the major.

"The one out in the desert that your men were fixin' to hoist onto that flatbed truck," said Jo-Jo.

"That wasn't a spacecraft, Jo-Jo. That was a weather balloon," said Major Paine. He turned to Marcel. "And who's this guy? Is he with you?"

"No, sir, Major Paine," said Marcel. "My name is Marcel Duchamp and I work at the Titanic Hotel in Vegas."

"Is that right?" said Major Paine. "Then what were you doing snooping around the, uh, weather balloon?"

"Well, sir, I've been tailing these kids because—"

Quick, Lek esped. *He is going to tell the major that we are aliens!*

"Major Paine, this man is not who he says," said Ploo. "He is a shape-changing alien from outer space!"

Marcel's face turned bright pink.

"It—it's not *me* who's the shape-changing alien," sputtered Marcel. "It's these *kids*! They cheated our casino out of thirty thousand dollars with some kind of alien tricks! My boss sent me to spy on them."

"That's ridiculous!" said Jo-Jo. "How could *kids* cheat a casino out of thousands of dollars? Major, these children are my sister Carol-Ann's kids from New York City, and I've known 'em since they was about yay high."

"What?" said Marcel, his face turning bright red.

"Ploo is right," said Klatu. "I saw this Marcel person change into a disgusting, huge-headed, big-eyed, gray-skinned monster with an ugly antenna growing right out of the middle of his head."

"He's lying!" screamed Marcel, his

face turning purple. "They're all lying!"

"Sir," said Lek, "what my brother Klatu said is not exactly the truth. The truth is mmllff—"

Ploo had clapped her hand over Lek's mouth to keep him from saying too much. He was always telling more of the truth than anyone wanted to hear.

"The truth is," said Ploo, "my brother Klatu was exaggerating. This Marcel person is not disgusting or ugly, but he *is* dangerous."

"Sergeant," said Major Paine, "put Mr. Duchamp into a holding cell and lock him up for further questioning."

The soldiers dragged Marcel out of the major's office, kicking and screaming.

Ploo leaned in close to Major Paine. "You can tell he is an alien by how he was kicking and screaming," she said. "I have heard that is what aliens do."

With Marcel out of his office, Major
Paine seemed to relax.

"You know," said the major to Ploo,
"my daughter Lily is just about your age.
Would you like to meet her?"

"Very much," said Ploo, smiling.

3

Meet Ploo— She's Not from Around Here

Major Paine picked up the phone and dialed his home.

"Lily, it's Daddy," said the major. "I have a surprise for you. An old friend of yours is here in my office." He winked at Jo-Jo. "No, I can't tell you who. It's a surprise. Yes, come right over."

When Lily walked into the major's office, the first person she saw was Jo-Jo. With a cry of joy, Lily flung herself right into the big blond mechanic's arms.

"Hi, darlin'!" said Jo-Jo, hugging the little girl. "So wonderful to see you!"

Major Paine waited for them to end their hug.

"And, Lily," said the major, "these are Jo-Jo's niece and nephews from back east. I'm sorry, kids, I'm not sure I remember all your names. The little girl's name was Pru, I think?"

"Not Pru. *Ploo,*" said Ploo.

Lily's eyes opened so wide, Ploo worried her eyeballs would fall out.

It is me, Lily, Ploo esped directly to Lily's mind. Pretend you are meeting me for the first time.

Lily could barely hide her excitement. "Nice to meet you, Ploo," said Lily.

"Aunt Jo-Jo was showing us around Nedava," said Klatu, looking at Jo-Jo.

Lek kicked him. *Nevada,* he esped.

"We were driving in the desert," Klatu continued, "and we came upon an alien spaceship—"

"He means a weather balloon," said Major Paine.

"No," said Ploo, "he means an alien spaceship. And these soldiers arrested us for trespassing."

"But we locked up this alien fellow, Marcel, so that's all cleared up now, isn't it?" said the major with a little laugh. "No hard feelings, I hope?"

"My feelings are not hard," said Lek.

"Good," said the major.

"Neither are mine," said Klatu. "I have only soft feelings."

Everybody laughed. They thought he was making a joke.

"So, Major," said Jo-Jo, "could you give

us a lift back to our car in the desert?"

The major frowned. "I can't spare any-body tonight," he said. "Not till morning."

"Can they stay with us tonight, Daddy?" asked Lily. "Ploo can sleep in *my* room."

"Well, kitten, I don't know," said the major.

"Oh, please, please, pretty please with sugar on it?" Lily begged.

The major smiled. "All right, sure, why not?" he said.

"Thank you, Daddy," said Lily. She kissed the major good night.

4

Eat Your Cookies and Milk—That's an Order!

"So, Ploo, did you like Las Vegas?" Lily asked.

The two little girls were lying on beds in Lily's bedroom. Lek and Klatu were in the guest room. Jo-Jo was sleeping on the living room couch. Ploo had just morphed back into her Looglish shape.

"I did not realize Earth cities are so small," said Ploo. "In Las Vegas, we saw Paris, Venice, and New York."

Lily giggled. "Those weren't the actual cities you saw, Ploo. They were just made to look like parts of them."

"Oh," said Ploo.

There was a knock on the door. Before Lily could answer, the door opened and Lily's mom came in. She was carrying a tray.

Ploo dove under the covers. *I hope Mrs. Paine did not see Lily talking to a huge-headed, velvety-soft, gray-skinned alien with gorgeous black eyes and a lovely antenna curling out of her head,* she thought.

"I brought you girls some milk and cookies," said Mrs. Paine. "Then it's lights-out, spit-spot." She frowned at the big lump in Ploo's bed. "Where's little Pru?" she asked.

"*Ploo,* not Pru," said Lily. "She's right there in her bed, Mom."

"Would you like some milk and cookies, Pru?" called Mrs. Paine.

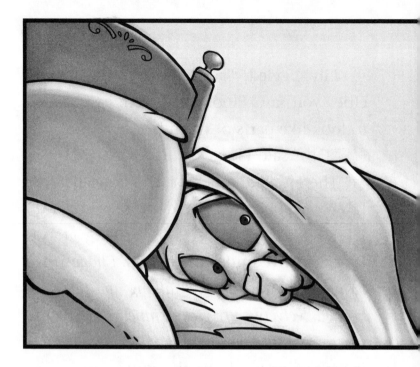

"Yes, thank you," called Ploo from under the covers. *I wonder what milk and cookies are,* she thought.

"Well, come out and get them, dear," called Mrs. Paine.

"I can not," said Ploo.

"Why can't you?" asked Mrs. Paine.

"She's just shy, Mom," said Lily. "Don't bug her."

"She wasn't shy when I met her an hour ago," said Mrs. Paine.

"Well, she is now," said Lily. "She . . . got a zit on her forehead."

"So fast?" said Mrs. Paine. "Let me see it, Pru. I have something that gets rid of zits."

Major Paine came into the bedroom. He seemed annoyed.

"What's all the discussion in here?" he

asked. "Some people in this house are trying to sleep."

Uh-oh, thought Ploo, *this is not good. If the major sees me in my lovely Looglish body, he will lock me up again! And this time not even Lily and Jo-Jo together can save me.*

"I brought the girls some milk and cookies, dear," said Mrs. Paine. "But little Pru won't come out from under the covers."

"That's ridiculous," said the major. "Pru, you come out here this instant and eat those cookies! That's an order!"

"Daddy, you can't give my friends orders," said Lily. "Ploo isn't one of your soldiers."

I wonder if I could slip into his mind and plant a few ideas, thought Ploo. She slid her antenna out from under the covers. She pointed it in the major's direction.

. . . nasty, badly behaved little brat, he

was thinking. *How dare she not come out for milk and cookies!*

"She'd better come out here and eat those cookies," said the major. "And why is she hiding under the covers, anyway? I don't like that."

Ploo grabbed the major's thought stream and followed it back into his mind. His thoughts were clenched tightly like angry fists, crowded together in orderly rows. What could she do with his foolish, angry thoughts?

Her mind gently squeezed the major's mind like a lump of clay. She loosened the tight coils. She messed up the neat rows. She pinched a little here, poked a little there.

. . . nice, well-behaved little girl, he was thinking. *I daresay she doesn't need to come out for milk and cookies. . . .*

"Lily says Pru's shy because she has a zit," said Mrs. Paine.

"Well, there must be an *outbreak* of zits," said the major, "because both her brothers are under the covers, too. Pru, I changed my mind. You don't have to come out for milk and cookies if you don't want to."

"Thank you, Major Paine," said Ploo. *And my name is Ploo, not Pru,* she thought, giving his mind a final squeeze.

"Good night, Lily," said the major. "Good night, Ploo."

"Good night, Major Paine," said Ploo.

"Her name is *Pru,*" said Mrs. Paine.

"No, it isn't," said the major.

Lily's mom and dad kissed Lily good night and left the room, closing the door behind them.

"Whew! That was a close one!" whispered

Lily. "I can't believe Daddy changed his mind so suddenly about the milk and cookies."

"*I* can," said Ploo. She giggled.

"Did you have something to do with that, Ploo?" Lily asked.

"Maybe a little," said Ploo.

5

Free Marcel!

Ploo and Lily ate the cookies and drank the milk.

"So, Ploo," said Lily when the last cookie was gone. "What do you want to do now?"

Ploo jumped off the bed and pushed up the bedroom window. "I want to go and find Marcel," she said. "We have to free him."

"Marcel?" said Lily. "Isn't he the alien my dad locked up?"

"No," Ploo answered. "Marcel works at the Titanic Hotel casino in Las Vegas. He was following us because he thinks we cheated him. I feel sorry for Marcel. It is my fault he is locked up in his cage. I hated it when they locked *me* up in a cage."

Lily shrugged. "Okay, Ploo," she said. "Let's go."

The two little girls climbed quietly out of Lily's bedroom window. They crept through the streets of Area 51. It was very late and very dark. The night bugs were still chirping and chattering, but not as loudly as before. Somewhere a coyote howled.

"I'm not sure this is such a good idea, Ploo," Lily whispered.

"Where are they holding Marcel?" asked Ploo.

"Follow me," said Lily.

The guardhouse looked blue-white in the moonlight. It was so quiet now that Ploo and Lily's soft footsteps on the gravel path sounded dangerously loud.

"This is probably where they're keeping him," said Lily.

There was a small window at the back of the guardhouse. Ploo could hear loud snoring. Lily boosted Ploo up onto a bench and they looked inside. The window had bars. The spaces between the bars were too small for a little girl to fit through, even a little alien girl.

Through the bars Ploo and Lily could see Marcel. He was lying asleep on a narrow cot. The door to his cell had tall steel bars in it. Not far from the cot, they could see a guard in a chair. His head was slumped forward. Like Marcel, he was fast asleep. Both of them were snoring loudly.

Their snuffling and snorting sounded more like barn animals than humans.

Ploo slid her antenna out of her head

and pointed it in Marcel's direction. She let her thoughts trickle into his head. *Wake up, Marcel,* she esped. *I want to speak to you.* Marcel continued to snore. *Wake up, Marcel— your pants are on fire!*

Marcel woke with a jolt. He gave a little cry, grabbed his butt, and jumped off the cot. He looked down at his pants and realized they weren't on fire.

"Hello, Marcel," said Ploo out loud. "It is me, Ploo. One of the kids you were following."

"What are *you* doing here?" he demanded.

"Shhhhh, you will wake the guard," Ploo whispered. "I came to set you free."

"What?"

"I felt bad that you are locked up," said Ploo. "If you promise to stop following us, I will set you free."

"Yeah, right," said Marcel. "Like you could actually do that."

"You have seen me turn into an elephant," said Ploo. "Do you think setting you free would be harder than that? What do you say, Marcel? If I let you out, will you leave us alone?"

"I guess so," said Marcel.

"Do you promise or do you not?"

"I promise, I promise, okay? Though I don't know what I'm going to tell the boss."

"Good," said Ploo.

She pointed her antenna at the sleeping guard. She let her thoughts trickle into his mind. He was dreaming about being in a restaurant. He was sitting at a table. A waitress with red hair was serving him a huge chocolate sundae with plenty of whipped cream and sprinkles on top.

Good evening, Ploo esped. What a pleasant dream you are having now. Only one thing could make it less than pleasant. That prisoner in your cell, Marcel. As long as he is in that cell, your dream could turn very ugly. Monsters might come to you in your dream. Would you like to see one of these monsters?

The red-haired waitress suddenly grew warts and horns and three-inch fangs.

The chocolate sundae was suddenly crawling with worms. The guard screamed in his sleep.

I could make the monster go away, Ploo esped. If you want it to go away, get up now, walk to his cell, and unlock the door.

Whimpering, the guard got unsteadily to his feet. Eyes still closed, he walked to the door of Marcel's cell and unlocked it. Eyes wide open, Marcel backed out of his cell.

The worms in the guard's dream disappeared. The waitress's warts, horns, and fangs disappeared. The guard stopped whimpering. He walked back to his chair and finished his chocolate sundae.

Marcel tiptoed out of the guardhouse. He met Ploo outside the door and shook her hand. "Thanks, kid," he said. "You're pretty nice for a big-eyed, grayskinned alien."

He pulled up the collar of his trench coat and vanished into the night.

Lily and Ploo sneaked back to Lily's house and crept inside.

6

How Cool Is Hangar 18?

Early-morning sunlight slanted across the grass. Klatu, Lek, Ploo, Lily, and Jo-Jo stood outside Hangar 18, a big boxy building. It was where alien spaceships that crashed in the Nevada desert were kept. Jo-Jo was carrying her toolbox.

"Now remember," whispered Jo-Jo as she unlocked the door of the gigantic tin building, "I never let you into Hangar 18, okay?"

"If you never let us in," said Klatu, "then who is letting us in?"

"I am," said Jo-Jo.

"You never let us in, but you are letting us in?" said Klatu. "I do not understand."

"She means not to tell anybody she's letting us in," said Lily.

"Oh," said Klatu. "Why did you not say so?"

Jo-Jo pulled the door open. She went in and turned on the lights. Klatu, Lek, Ploo, and Lily followed her.

Klatu gasped when he saw what was inside the hangar. Nearly a dozen weird-looking spaceships filled the huge room. There were saucer-shaped ships, cigar-shaped ships, ball-shaped ships, and ships that were shaped like big brass bells. Some spaceships were wrecked and in pieces, but most of them looked like they could fly.

"Look," said Klatu. "It is a Mardoolian Bonklebob!" He pointed to a shiny red pancake-shaped spaceship with white wings.

"Where did these ships come from?" asked Lily.

"All over the universe, I expect," said Jo-Jo.

"That one over there looks Looglish, but from a long time ago," said Ploo. "I remember seeing one like it in our history books."

"You probably did, hon," said Jo-Jo. "It's one of the ships that crashed in Roswell, New Mexico."

"Over there in the corner!" cried Klatu. "It is our spaceship!"

"Right," said Jo-Jo. "Time to do some tinkering. I'll fix the anti-gravs, the landing ring, and a couple other doodads." She picked up her toolbox and headed for the corner. The kids followed. "After I'm done

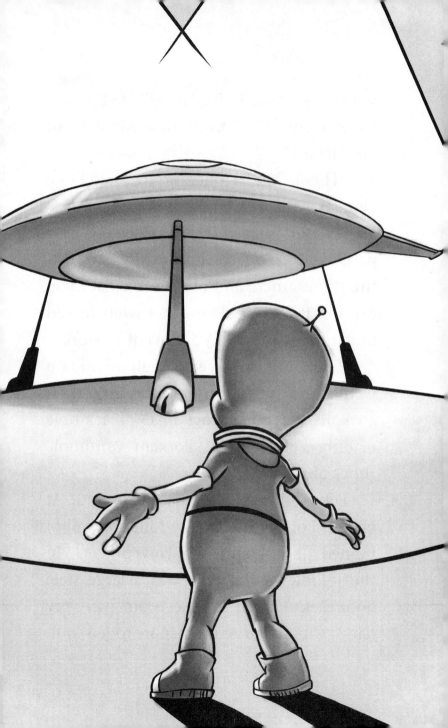

with this," said Jo-Jo, "it will give you a sweeter ride than even that Mardoolian Bonklebob."

"Thank you so much, Jo-Jo," said Ploo. "We are very grateful."

"Gettin' that thing fixed is the easy part," said Jo-Jo. "The hard part will be gettin' it outta here and off to someplace you can use it." She pulled out a wrench, slid under the ship's belly, and went to work.

Ploo and Lily stayed to help her. Klatu went from ship to ship, peering into their cockpits, saying things like "black-hole reading lights!" and "Zorkian wormhole shock absorbers!"

Lek wandered off to look around. At one end of the hangar, he found a wall of framed photographs of army officers. In the middle of the wall was a large steel door. Lek opened it. The room was very dark. Clouds of cold vapor rolled out.

Machinery somewhere inside the room hummed loudly. Lek entered the dark, freezing room.

"Klatu, Ploo, Lily, Jo-Jo!" he shouted a minute later. "Come quick!" They came running.

"What is it? I can't see a thing," said Jo-Jo. "On the wall near the doorway is a control panel with light switches. Would one of y'all turn on the lights?" Darksider Looglings could see perfectly in the dark.

"*I* shall do it," said Klatu. He began throwing switches, but the lights didn't come on. The humming sound grew louder.

"Can't you find the lights?" said Jo-Jo.

The lights came on, blinding them for a moment.

"That's better," said Jo-Jo.

The freezer room was caked in frost. Icicles hung from pipes in the ceiling. There were several steel barrels near a wall. In the middle of the room were half a dozen big glass tubes. The pipes in the ceiling ran into the tops of the tubes. Inside the tubes stood four bodies. Four bodies with enormous black eyes, gray skin, and antennae growing out of their huge heads.

"They are Looglings!" cried Ploo.

"They've been there forever, darlin'," said Jo-Jo. "They came from that UFO crash in Roswell."

"If they are from Roswell," said Ploo, "then they are the Great Ones!"

"The Great Ones!" said Lek. "They will stand forever as a grim memorial to Looglish heroism!"

Ploo, Lek, and Klatu broke into the well-known Looglish cheer for the four aliens who'd crashed at Roswell, New Mexico:

"Threes and twos and ones and zeroes!
Name our bravest Looglish heroes!
Darkside, Lightside, all agree
Who'll go down in history:
Org and Murkel, Shemp and Kurth
Found semi-intelligent life on Earth!
Sis boom bam! Sis boom zest!
Great Ones, Great Ones, you're the best!"

While they were singing, the humming sound grew softer, then stopped altogether.

"What happened?" asked Jo-Jo. "Klatu, which switches did you throw?"

"I did not throw anything," said Klatu.

"I think he threw the switch that turns off the freezers," said Lily.

"I did not throw the switch," said Klatu. "And if I threw it, I could not have thrown it far."

Klatu flipped more switches. A mechanical whirring sound started softly and grew louder. An alarm began to screech. Clouds of vapor poured out of the pipes into the glass tubes. Now there was so much vapor inside the tubes that the kids could no longer see the bodies.

"Klatu, what did you do now?" asked Jo-Jo.

"Nothing! I did nothing!"

"You turned on the heating system!" said Jo-Jo. "The heat is on full blast! Tarnation, Klatu!"

Jo-Jo went to the control panel and threw more switches. The alarm stopped screeching. Slowly, the vapor faded and disappeared. Water streamed down the insides of the tubes.

"Oh no! They're thawing out!" said Jo-Jo. "The bodies are melting!"

"Klatu, you *varna*!" said Lek. "You have melted the Great Ones! Now they will no longer stand forever as a grim memorial to Looglish heroism."

"I have done nothing!" said Klatu. "The Great Ones are still great! See? They are just as before. They are not melting. They are—"

"Moving," said Ploo.

"They *are* moving," said Lily. She shivered, but not from the cold.

"They are *not* moving," said Lek. "They are *dead*. How could they be moving?"

"Look," said Jo-Jo. "Did y'all see that? That hand actually moved."

Everybody leaned in close to the tube to see.

"It did move," said Ploo. "I saw it move!"

It was true. The fingers on the hand of one of the bodies were twitching.

Now all four of the bodies were beginning to move. Fingers. Feet. Faces. Hands reached out to the glass around them and tried to push it open.

"They are *alive*!" said Lek. "The Great Ones are *alive*!"

"They want to get out!" said Ploo. "Let them out!"

"Do you think it is safe to let them out?" asked Lek.

Jo-Jo sprang to the doors of the tubes.

One by one, she unlocked the doors and
flung them open. The Great Ones seemed
dazed. They held out their arms. They
stretched out their legs. They stumbled out
of the tubes and staggered around like
zombies. They stumbled into each other
and fell down. They got up again.

"They should be called the Clumsy
Ones," Klatu whispered in Lek's ear-hole.

Are you Org, Murkel, Shemp, and Kurth? **Ploo esped.**

Yes! **esped a deep voice.** How did you know our names?

Sir, you are famous on planet Loogl, **Klatu esped.** On Loogl you are known as the Great Ones.

Do you know about planet Loogl?

Sir, we <u>come</u> from planet Loogl, **Ploo esped.** A short time ago, three of us came here to do extra-credit science projects for school, and we crash-landed.

Sir, it was not so much a <u>crash</u> landing as a <u>hard</u> landing, **esped Klatu.**

You are saying that you come from planet Loogl? **esped another deep voice.**

Yes! **Ploo esped.**

Funny, you do not <u>look</u> Looglish.

That is because I am not the tall yellow-haired creature, **Ploo esped. She waved.** I am over here. Those awful-looking creatures are humans, not Looglings. They are our friends.

"What's going on?" asked Jo-Jo. "Are you talking to them by E.S.P.?"

"Uh, right," said Ploo. She felt bad about calling humans awful-looking, even though they were. Tiny, beady little eyes. Laughably small heads. Yucky pink skin. Ugh!

"What are the Great Ones saying?" asked Jo-Jo.

"That you do not look Looglish," said Ploo.

"Well, duh," said Jo-Jo.

There was a noise at the front door of the hangar. Everybody froze.

"What was that?" Klatu whispered.

"Somebody is trying to get in the front door!" Lily whispered.

"We are doomed!" whispered Lek.

Where Is Here?

Jo-Jo moved quickly. She pulled the freezer door shut. She pushed the Great Ones into hiding places behind the large steel barrels. She motioned for Lily, Ploo, Lek, and Klatu to hide there, too. They crouched behind the barrels. They waited and listened.

What is happening? esped another deep voice.

Sir, a human is coming into the building, esped Ploo. If it finds us here, it will be very bad for us.

50

Where is here? esped the voice.

We are in Area 51, sir, a secret human army base in Nevada, Lek told him.

We crashed a few days ago in a place called Roswell, New Mexico, esped the voice of one of the Great Ones. *We must recover our spaceship and repair it before the humans find it.*

Sir, you did not crash a few days ago, esped Lek. *You crashed almost sixty human years ago.*

Sixty human years! esped the voice. *I find that unlikely. And what happened to our spaceship?*

Your spaceship was found, sir, esped Lek, *but it cannot be repaired. You are doomed.*

Ploo glared at Lek across the darkness. *You are not doomed, sir,* she esped. *You are never doomed when you have friends. We will help you.*

Well, then, be quick about it, esped the voice. *We cannot wait forever.*

Yes, esped another voice, *we are very important Darksiders. We must not be kept waiting as if we were common Lightsiders.*

It was icy cold in the room. Jo-Jo wrapped her arms around Lily to keep her warm. The Looglings weren't bothered by the cold, but Ploo put one of Jo-Jo's arms around herself, anyway. And then one of Lily's. All three of them hugged.

The front door of the hangar finally opened. Somebody came in.

"Who's in here?" a voice demanded.

Klatu and Lek and Ploo looked at each other, their eyes wide. Lek looked like he was going to die of fright.

"Anybody here?" the voice called.

Jo-Jo and the kids were absolutely silent.

It was very cold in the freezer room. Ploo, Lek, and Klatu could see the humans' breath in the frigid air. They waited in silence. Time ticked slowly by with no sound from outside the room. The suspense was unbearable.

Suddenly the freezer room door was yanked open.

"Anybody in here?" said a voice.

Jo-Jo and the kids stopped breathing.

"Can't see a thing in here," muttered the voice. "Where the heck are the lights?"

They could hear somebody feeling around on the wall, looking for the light switch. If the lights went on now, it would be very bad.

"It's too dark to even find the switches," said the voice. "And it's freezing. I'd better go get me a flashlight and a sweater."

Footsteps walked to the door. The door slammed behind them. Then there was a click. It was the sound of the door being locked.

"Uh-oh," said Lily.

"Friends," said Jo-Jo, "we got us about five minutes to find a way out of here before that clown comes back. And before we freeze to death."

"Oh, was that a clown?" asked Klatu excitedly. "I have always wanted to see a clown! I *love* a clown!"

"In English, *clown* sometimes means '*varna,*'" said Lily.

"Ah," said Klatu. "I knew that."

Jo-Jo was feeling around on the wall for the light switch.

"Let me turn on the lights," said Ploo. "I can see in the dark."

Ploo walked to the switches and turned on the lights.

When will we be given a spaceship so that we may leave this place? esped a deep voice. *We are tired of waiting.*

Sir, we are locked inside this freezer, and the human is coming back, Ploo esped. Ploo was trying to control her temper. *These Great Ones are not so great,* she thought. *Maybe they should be called the Annoying Ones instead.*

Jo-Jo examined the door. There didn't seem to be a way to unlock it from the inside.

"How are we going to get out of here?" asked Lily.

"That I do not know, little darlin'," said Jo-Jo.

"Are we doomed?" asked Lek.

"I wouldn't say we're doomed, hon, but things aren't lookin' too rosy," said Jo-Jo.

"Maybe I can try something," said Ploo.

"Be my guest, darlin'," said Jo-Jo.

Ploo slid her antenna out of her head and pointed it toward the lock. Then she let her thoughts seep into the door and dribble into the lock. She found she could see the insides of the lock, just like the insides of the minds she slipped into. It was a different kind of lock than the one on her cage the time they captured her. She tugged at a piece of metal here. She pushed at a piece of metal there. She slid a piece of metal along a track.

Everybody in the room heard a click. Then another. Then the lock snapped open.

"You did it!" said Lily.

Ploo, Lek, Klatu, Lily, Jo-Jo, Org, Murkel, Shemp, and Kurth crept out of the freezer and into the hangar. Jo-Jo shut the freezer room door behind them.

. In this hangar I see many spacecraft from many planets, esped a deep voice. Which one shall we use to return to Loogl?

. Sir, you cannot just steal a spaceship and fly back to Loogl, Lek esped.

Why not? esped the voice.

58

It is wrong to steal, sir, Lek esped.

It may be wrong for others, esped the voice. It is not wrong for us. Are we not the Great Ones? You said it yourself.

"Okay, gang," said Jo-Jo. "Before we mosey on out of here, I suggest you and your buddies morph into human shape. Can they do that?"

What sort of ship did you use to get here from Loogl? esped the deep voice.

It is the small silver one against the far wall, esped Klatu.

That tiny thing in the shape of a saucer? esped the voice.

Yes, sir, esped Klatu.

Well, it looks like a ship for children, esped the voice. But it will do. The voice sighed loudly.

"Ploo, ask your pals if they can morph into human shape," said Jo-Jo. "We better move fast. That soldier might come back any minute now."

"All right," said Ploo. Sirs, do you know how to morph into human shape? she esped. If so, you must do it right away.

Of course we know how to morph into human shape, esped the deep voice. Do you think we are <u>varnas</u>? What sort of Earth clothing should we be wearing when we morph?

Klatu pointed to the framed photographs on the wall. They were pictures of army generals from the 1950s.

Those are human soldiers, Klatu esped. Try looking like them.

Good, esped the voice.

The Great Ones grew taller and heavier. Their heads and eyes shrank. Their skin grew so pink, they looked like they'd just spent the day at the beach. Lek, Ploo, and Klatu morphed, too.

No sooner had they finished morphing than the front door of the hangar swung open. Jo-Jo shooed Ploo, Lily, Lek, Klatu, Org, Murkel, Shemp, and Kurth behind the taller spaceships.

Two soldiers entered, carrying flash-lights.

"I heard somebody in here earlier," said one of the soldiers.

"Let's check the freezer room," said the other soldier.

They crept up to the door. The first soldier threw it open and shone his flashlight inside. Then he went into the freezer room and turned on the lights.

"They're gone!" he shouted. "The frozen alien bodies are all gone!"

The second soldier rushed into the freezer room. "You're right!" he said. "The alien bodies have been stolen! We have to find the thieves!"

The soldiers dashed back into the hangar and began looking between the spaceships. They ran smack into Ploo, Lek, Klatu, Lily, Jo-Jo, Org, Murkel, Shemp, and Kurth, who were crouching behind a tall, cigar-shaped craft.

For a moment, everyone was so surprised, nobody spoke. Then the two soldiers saw the Great Ones' uniforms and realized they were standing in front of army generals. Right away, they came to attention and snapped their right hands to their foreheads in a military salute.

The Great Ones seemed confused. They smiled goofy smiles and remained crouching.

"*Sirs*, begging your pardon, *sirs*!" said the first soldier. "Why are you generals crouching behind this spacecraft, sirs?"

"They were . . . playing hide-and-seek," said Lily.

"Who were they hiding from?" asked the second soldier.

"Other generals," said Lily.

The soldiers frowned.

They do not believe this, esped Lek. *They know that the Great Ones are not human generals!*

"Sirs," said the first soldier, "do either Major Paine or General Stinkfellow know you gentlemen are on the base?"

"Major Paine knows *we're* here," said Lek. "He may not know about the generals."

"And this is because . . . ?" said the second soldier.

"Because they're on a top-secret mission," said Lily.

"They're on a top-secret mission . . . playing hide-and-seek?" said the second soldier.

"It's part of . . . war games," said Jo-Jo.

"Uh-huh," said the second soldier. "All right, ma'am, I'm going to have to ask all of you to come with us to Major Paine."

I told you they do not believe us, **Lek esped.** *Major Paine will not only find out that the Great Ones are aliens, he will also find out about us. We are all doomed!*

8

General Confusion

"Well, hello there," said Major Paine as Lily, Jo-Jo, Lek, Ploo, and Klatu came through the door of his office. "Are you enjoying your visit?"

Then the soldiers brought in Org, Murkel, Shemp, and Kurth. Major Paine jumped to his feet, stood at attention, and gave them a military salute.

"Tell them to return the salute," Jo-Jo whispered to Ploo. "Tell them to raise their hand quickly to their face and then drop."

Jo-Jo says raise your hand quickly to your face and then drop, esped Ploo.

Org, Murkel, Shemp, and Kurth whipped their hands to their faces so quickly, they smacked themselves in the nose. Then they dropped to the floor.

I do not think that is what Jo-Jo meant by dropping, esped Ploo. *Get up fast!*

The Great Ones struggled to their feet, grinning goofy smiles.

"Generals, it's an honor to have you here," said the major. "And a surprise. What brings you to Area 51?"

Quick! esped Lek. *Somebody give them language gum!*

Ploo, Lek, and Klatu searched in their pockets for language gum balls.

I have some! esped Klatu. Without stopping to look at their colors, Klatu slipped gum balls into the hands of each of the Great Ones.

Sirs, these gum balls are language gum, Klatu esped. *Chew fast and you will be able to talk to him!*

The Great Ones chewed quickly. Kurth was the first to speak.

"*Buenos días*," said Kurth. That was "Good day" in Spanish.

"*Guten Tag*," said Shemp. That was "Good day" in German.

"*Kalimera*," said Org. That was "Good morning" in Greek.

"*God dag*," said Murkel. That was "Good day" in Norwegian.

Klatu, you varna! esped Lek. What color gum balls did you give them?

Major Paine frowned. "What language are you gentlemen speaking?" he asked.

"These officers were stationed all over the world," said Jo-Jo. "They were just showing you some of the countries they've served in."

"I see," said Major Paine. He examined their uniforms and frowned. "Why are you gentlemen in uniforms that have not been worn in fifty years?" he asked.

Ploo and Lily looked at each other in panic. They didn't realize the photos the Great Ones had copied before morphing were of generals from so long ago. The major's question hung in the air like cigar smoke. Nobody could think of an answer.

"There's a very simple reason for that, Daddy," Lily blurted. She didn't know what she would say next. She just knew somebody had to say *something.*

"Really, kitten?" said Major Paine. "Well, what is it?"

Lily's mind raced through many crazy explanations. None of them made sense. Everybody in the room was staring at her, waiting.

"Daddy, these generals . . . were abducted by aliens fifty years ago," said Lily finally. "The aliens who landed here the other night brought them back. That's why they seem kind of weird. If *you'd* spent the last fifty years on an alien planet, you'd probably be acting weird, too."

Jo-Jo flashed her a secret thumbs-up sign. Everybody relaxed.

"Ah, that explains it," said the major. He waved to the two soldiers who were standing by the window. "Well, gentle-men, welcome to Area 51. My men will take you to the washroom to freshen up.

But then I want to hear all about your abduction!"

When they left Major Paine's office, everyone congratulated Lily on her fast thinking.

"How did you ever come up with something so clever?" Ploo asked.

Lily blushed. "I don't know," she said. "But you guys were great, too."

"Everybody but Klatu," said Lek. "Klatu, where in the universe did you get so many gum balls of the wrong color?"

"I did not notice *you* giving them the right-color ones," said Klatu.

"There is only one problem now," said Lek. "In one *arp,* the Great Ones will morph back into Looglings." He looked at his *arp*-timer. "No, in *less* than one *arp*. In just twenty-seven *mynts*."

"There is another problem," said Ploo. "The Great Ones want to come back to Loogl with us in our spaceship."

"But there is not room for both them and us!" said Lek.

"Exactly," said Ploo. "If we give them our spaceship, then we are stranded here on Earth."

"And doomed," Lek added.

"How could we refuse them?" said Klatu. "They are the Great Ones."

"But they're so rude," said Lily. "I'd call them the Rude Ones. I wouldn't give them anything."

"I do not like them very much," said Ploo, "but Klatu is right. They are the Great Ones. They are heroes to every Loogling in the universe. If they want to borrow our spaceship, I am afraid we cannot say no."

9

Kick the Tires and Take It for a Spin

When the Great Ones came back from the washroom, they looked strange. Some kind of foam was coming out of Org's mouth. Murkel had shaving cream on his forehead. Kurth had his officer's jacket on backward. Shemp had toothpaste in his hair.

"Major Paine, sir," said one of the soldiers, "the generals don't speak English at all. And they don't seem to know how to wash up."

"Well, let's not be too tough on them,"

said Major Paine. "We can't *imagine* what kind of torture those aliens put them through, poor devils."

"*Buenos días,*" said Kurth.

"*Guten Tag,*" said Shemp.

"*Kalimera,*" said Org.

"*God dag,*" said Murkel.

"Absolutely, gentlemen," said Major Paine. "Absolutely."

"You know," said Jo-Jo, "I don't rightly think the generals are goin' to be tellin' us much about what happened to them when they were prisoners of the aliens. But I bet they could sure show us a thing or two about those alien spacecraft we've rebuilt."

"Hmmm, interesting idea," said the major.

"Why not haul some of those babies out of the hangar and ask the generals to put them through their paces?" asked Jo-Jo.

The major thought this over.

"Well, they probably know a heck of a lot more about how those things work than *we* do," said the major.

"I reckon they do," said Jo-Jo.

"Yes, I'm glad I thought of it," said the major. "Men, let's roll a few of those—heh heh—'weather balloons' out of the hangar. The generals are going to take one or two of them for a spin to show us how they work."

"Yes, sir," said one of the soldiers.

The Bonklebob! Klatu esped. Take the Mardoolian Bonklebob!

Sometimes he wished he could mold humans' thoughts like Ploo.

Ten minutes later, the soldiers had moved several spacecraft outside, including a long, cigar-shaped one, the kids' saucer-shaped one, and one that looked like a giant Slinky toy.

The Great Ones stumbled toward the hangar. They didn't look good. Their eyes had definitely grown bigger. So had their heads. Their skin was a good deal grayer than before. And Ploo saw the beginnings of antennae sprouting out of their heads. Had Major Paine noticed these changes?

Why are they morphing out of their human shapes so soon? Lek esped. They morphed human less than an arp ago.

Maybe it has something to do with being frozen for all those years, Ploo esped.

Lek looked nervously at his *arp*-timer. At the rate they are morphing, they will return to alien shape in no more than two mynts. What will happen to them then? What will happen to us?

"All right, gentlemen," said the major. "These are some of the spacecraft we've picked up at alien crash landings. If any of them remind you of ships you saw when

you were abducted, please enter them now."

Great Ones, esped Klatu, if you would like to try out our spaceship, it is the saucer-shaped silver one.

Org, Murkel, Shemp, and Kurth stumbled toward the kids' spaceship and climbed inside.

"Amazing," said Major Paine. "They don't speak English anymore, and yet they clearly understood me. Well, I've always been able to communicate with military men."

This spacecraft is hardly big enough for four grown Looglings, esped a deep voice. They will laugh at us on planet Loogl when we get out of it.

Sirs, **esped Ploo,** we are lending you our spacecraft on two conditions. One: that as soon as you get to Loogl, you send someone back to Earth with a bigger ship to rescue us. And two: that you be polite for the first time since we met you and thank us for the huge favor we are granting you.

Which of you Looglings dares to speak to the Great Ones in such a rude tone? **esped a deep and angry voice.**

Klatu, Lek, and Ploo shuddered with fear. It was me, Ploo, **esped Ploo, standing up as straight as she could.**

One of the Great Ones—it was hard to tell which, because by now he'd completely changed back to alien form—stuck his head out of the port and glared at Ploo.

"What the . . . ?" gasped Major Paine. "What the heck is wrong with that man's head?"

Well, Ploo, you are a very brave girl, esped the Looglish voice. And I apologize for all of us. Thank you for the spacecraft. We shall send back a bigger ship as soon as possible. Farewell! Looglings laroosh loglaroohoo!

"Hey," said Major Paine, "that creature *is* an alien! Stop them, men! Capture them before they escape!"

Several soldiers rushed toward the spaceship. The port closed. The first two soldiers reached the spacecraft and got a grip on its edge. The craft began to glow. The soldiers screamed and let go fast.

Without a sound, the craft rose straight up and hung for a moment over the hangar. Then it shot away into the bright sky and disappeared.

"Well, I'll be a monkey's aunt," said Jo-Jo.

"I was right!" shouted Major Paine. "I *knew* they were aliens!"

"Gosh, Daddy," said Lily. "I never even suspected."

"Who will ever believe we met real, live aliens!" said Ploo.

"I hope we do not catch some terrible alien virus from them," said Lek.

"Major Paine," said Klatu, "I have suddenly begun missing my home in Now Yerk. Is it possible that we might get a ride to our car in the desert as quickly as possible?"

10

Goodbye, Box Turtle Boy

The long pink Cadillac turned onto the main street of the little town of Groom Lake. It glided up to the curb outside Aldo's Pizza. Jo-Jo stayed behind the wheel, but Lek, Klatu, and Ploo got out of the car. They had morphed into human shape for this stop. Klatu pulled one big bag of money out of the trunk, and all three kids walked into the pizza store.

Klatu, quick—I have forgotten the name of the flat boxy things they sell here, **Lek esped.**

Box turtles, esped Klatu.

Not box turtles, esped Ploo. *Pizza,*

"May I help you?" asked the teenage boy behind the counter. He was the same boy whose station wagon Lek and Klatu had borrowed when they first came to Groom Lake. Unfortunately, they'd never gotten around to returning it.

"Oh. Yes," said Lek. "If you are the boy who delivers the box turt—"

"—who delivers the pizza—" said Ploo.

"—who delivers the pizza," said Lek, "then we have something for you."

He and Klatu lifted the heavy sack of money onto the counter.

"What's this?" asked the boy.

"I do not know," said Lek. "Perhaps money that somebody won in a casino."

The boy opened the sack, saw all the money, and gasped.

"Where did you get this?" he asked.

"From a friend," said Ploo.

"From a stranger," said Klatu. "He said this is to pay you back for borrowing your car and not returning it."

The boy looked shocked.

"You talked to the guy who stole our station wagon?" he said.

"Yes," said Ploo.

"No!" said Klatu.

"To tell you the absolute honest truth," said Lek, "we mmmlllfff—"

Klatu had clapped his hand over Lek's mouth. He didn't want to hear the absolute honest truth. "We have no idea what this money is, or who gave it to us, or why," said Klatu. "Goodbye, box turtle boy."

Lek, Ploo, and Klatu ran out of the pizza store and jumped into the pink Cadillac before the boy could say anything more.

Read on for a passage from
the fourth exciting book in
the weird planet series!

Finally the Elvises got ready to leave the casino. Klatu, Lek, Ploo, Lily, and Jo-Jo followed them downstairs to the Doo-Wop Mall. There the Elvises seemed to vanish.

"Where did they go?" Lek whispered.

Klatu, Lek, and Ploo looked all around. The mall was eerie and empty of tourists. Ploo could barely make out the statues of the rock stars. Lek was right—it was spooky to see them moving in the nearly dark mall.

As Jo-Jo and Lily passed by, the statues of the Beatles suddenly came to life. Paul and George grabbed Lily and Jo-Jo. Ringo tore off his mop-top wig. Under it was a black pompadour and sideburns. It was the evil Elvises!

Lily screamed. Jo-Jo punched out at them. It didn't work. Even when Klatu, Lek, and Ploo tried to help, it was hopeless. There were just too few Looglings and too many Elvises.

Judith Greenburg

About the Author

Dan Greenburg has written everything from books and magazine articles to advertisements, plays, and movie scripts. But his favorite work is writing for kids, and he's had otherworldly success with popular series such as The Zack Files. Dan lives with his wife, author J. C. Greenburg, and his son, Zack, in a house on the Hudson River, which they share with several cats.